TEEN

Culture & Leisure Services
Red Doles Lane
Huddersfield, West Yorks HD2 1YF

This book should be returned on or before the latest date stamped below. *Fines are charged if the item is late.*

You may renew this loan for a further period by phone, letter, personal visit or at www.kirklees.gov.uk/libraries, provided that the book is not required by another reader.

NO MORE THAN THREE RENEWALS ARE PERMITTED

en by
Zachary Sherman

ated by
ef Cage

red by
lon Iligan

D1362872

DEDICATED TO THE MEN AND WOMEN
OF THE ARMED FORCES

Raintree is an imprint of Capstone Global Library Limited,
a company incorporated in England and Wales having its
registered office at 7 Pilgrim Street, London, EC4V 6LB -
Registered company number: 6695582

To contact Raintree, please phone 0845 6044371,
fax + 44 (0) 1865 312263,
or email myorders@raintreepublishers.co.uk.

First published by Stone Arch Books © 2012
First published in the United Kingdom in 2013
The moral rights of the proprietor have been asserted.

Editor: Vaarunika Dharmapala
Art Director: Bob Lentz
Graphic Designer: Brann Garvey
Production Specialist: Michelle Biedscheid

ISBN 978 1 406 26193 6 (paperback)
17 16 15 14 13
10 9 8 7 6 5 4 3 2 1

British Library Cataloguing in Publication Data
A full catalogue record for this book is available from the British Library.

CONTENTS

PERSONNEL FILE

Lieutenant Commander
LESTER DONOVAN

ORGANIZATION:
US Navy SEALs

ENTERED SERVICE AT:
Naval Amphibious Base Coronado in
San Diego, CA,USA

BORN:
15th April 1972

EQUIPMENT

protective goggles

bulletproof vest

M4 carbine

ammo belt

M1911 pistol

first-aid pouch

Karambit knife

combat boots

OVERVIEW: WAR IN IRAQ

In 2002, the UN Security Council passed Resolution 1441, forcing Iraq to comply with the UN in a search for weapons of mass destruction (WMDs) in Iraqi facilities. The Iraqi government complied, allowing the UN Monitoring, Verification, and Inspection Commission (UNMOVIC) complete access to their country. However, the UNMOVIC was unable to locate any evidence of WMDs, and a US-run Iraqi survey group determined that all of Iraq's nuclear, chemical, and biological programmes had ended by 1991. Despite these findings, the invasion was undertaken on 20th March 2003, by order of the US President, George W. Bush and the UK Prime Minister, Tony Blair.

MAP

MISSION

Lieutenant Commander Lester Donovan and the US Navy SEALs must capture a known terrorist near the border of Syria.

CHAPTER 001

SURVIVING THE GAME

"This dustbowl is the armpit of humanity, if you ask me," a deep voice growled from the back seat of an armoured Humvee. The vehicle cut quickly from one lane to the next. The driver did his best to swerve in and out of the traffic that blocked their paths.

Traffic congestion in that part of Iraq was the stuff of legends. The men of 2nd Platoon, SEAL Team Two had become masters in the art of the "Slalom Slide", an unofficial driving manoeuvre that felt like a high-stakes video game. The team zigged and zagged around cars and pedestrians, bypassing the wretched bottleneck.

In the front seat, Lieutenant Commander Lester Donovan grimaced. He turned to face the man in the back seat. "What's your problem, Agent Upton?" the lieutenant asked.

Holding on to the headrest in front of him for support, Special Agent Bradley Upton, CIA, narrowed his eyes. He glared at Donovan. Upton's long face was boyish, hiding the fact that he was pushing forty years old. "What do you think?" Agent Upton said angrily. "These people ... all they do is blow themselves up. And for what? To make others conform to their way of thinking."

Petty Officer Kaili, the team's corpsman, had been sitting next to Upton for an hour, listening to him complain. "They've just installed democracy in this country," Kaili finally spoke up. "You gotta give it come time, bro. Give them a chance to do something with it."

"Whatever," Upton grumbled. "They've been killing their own people for hundreds of years. Nothing we do is going to change that. Murdering innocent civilians to make a point isn't part of the democratic process. It's terrorism. And that's why I'm stuck out here in the hot desert sand and not back home in Washington."

The driver, Master Chief Petty Officer Miller, was the team's explosive expert. He was also the oldest member of the platoon. Taking his eyes off the road for a moment, Miller angrily glared at Upton.

"If it wasn't for CIA guys like you, funding all the secret wars back in the 80s," said Miller, "we probably wouldn't be here either, College Boy."

"All right, Master Chief, knock it off," Donovan said. He looked down at his handheld GPS tracking unit.

"Where we going anyway, sir?" Miller asked Donovan.

"To see the –" Donovan began.

Upton promptly cut him off. "You'll know when I decide to tell you, Master Chief," said the CIA agent. "Until then? I suggest you shut up and drive!"

Miller turned and whispered to Donovan. "This guy's really starting to get on my nerves, sir," he said.

"That makes two of us, Master Chief," Donovan whispered back.

"Okay, let's look alive," said Miller, as the Humvee rolled into a new part of the city.

To his left, Donovan could see a pair of legs sticking straight up from the Humvee's floorboards behind him. Donovan tugged on the man's camos. "How's it look topside, Williams?" asked the lieutenant commander.

Seaman Second Class Williams, the team's sniper, stood in the Humvee's turret. The upper half of his body stuck out of a small hole in the vehicle's roof.

Williams's Nomex-gloved hands were wrapped around the massive .50-calibre machine gun, which was anchored on top of the Humvee. "Quiet as church on Sunday, sir," he yelled back down through the hole. Then he rotated the turret 180 degrees, scanning the area for signs of danger.

The heavy vehicle swung left, kicking up dust from its tyres. The two-lane road narrowed as the Humvee passed through a small alley. Then the road quickly opened into an expansive courtyard, nearly the size of a football field.

In this neighbourhood, the typical tan and beige tones of desert buildings suddenly gave way to more lively colours such as salmon and turquoise.

"Whoa!" Miller said. He whistled, impressed.

"Yeah, this is different," Kaili said, looking around at the unusually clean and lively streets.

Indeed it was.

The streets and shopfronts were free of rubbish, litter, and graffiti. The locals appeared to be orderly and polite. They waved at the soldiers and smiled as the Humvee cruised down the street.

"I don't care if people here are as nice as your momma back home," said Donovan. His eyes narrowed, scanning the area for the enemy. Usually when things got too quiet, he knew, trouble wasn't far behind. "Everyone stay frosty."

"Hey, spook!" Master Chief Miller shouted at Agent Upton over the hum of the 6.6-litre diesel engine.

Glowering over at Miller, Upton sneered. He obviously didn't like the term "spook", even though it was befitting his post. After all, he was a non-official government agent in the field, a cloak-and-dagger operative who made top-secret decisions from the shadows. Officially, he wasn't in Iraq. He was, in a sense, a ghost.

"How 'bout you tell us where we're headed?" said Miller. "What is this place? It's like the Twilight Zone."

"Fine," said Upton. "Police Chief Barana Hakedam, ex-warlord turned police magistrate, runs this area."

"Looks like he's done a bang-up job," Donovan said.

"Make no bones about it," replied Agent Upton. "He's an old Ba'athist supporter."

"Saddam Hussein's old ruling party?" asked Master Chief Miller.

"The one and only," Upton said, signalling Williams to stop the Humvee up ahead. "Police Chief Hakedam patrols these streets with an iron fist. His brothers are his deputies, and he trusts no one else. Hakedam says blood is the only thing that matters."

"Seems like a nice guy," Kaili joked. "But why are we going to see him?"

Agent Upton hesitated for a moment. "He has information he's willing to trade for the whereabouts of Abdul Kasieem," he finally said.

"King Commerce Kasieem?" Miller asked, recognizing the name from military debriefings.

"So you can read?" Upton said, laughing.

Miller held his breath, holding back his anger.

"I don't care who you are in the real world," said the Master Chief. "Talk to me like that again, and you'll go back to Washington, all right ... in a box."

"Don't test me," the CIA agent shot back. "I can have you erased, if you know what I mean."

Miller cracked a small smile. He nodded back at Upton, letting their differences go for the time being.

"Then as you know, Abdul Kasieem is the number one black marketer in the entire Middle East," Upton continued. "If we get our hands on him –"

"We put a major dent in the weapons-smuggling business around here," Donovan finished.

"Finally," Miller said. "A mission that makes sense!"

On the next street corner stood a large, imposing Iraqi man. He was well over six feet tall, weighed about two hundred pounds, and wore a dark green and khaki uniform. It was Barana Hakedam.

Opening the front door, Donovan stepped out and opened his palms. *"As-Salamu Alaykum,"* Donovan said, greeting the Iraqi police chief.

A smile swept across Hakedam's face. His pearly white teeth shone in the morning sun. "My friends! *Marhaban!*" Hakedam exclaimed. The police chief raised his arms in the air, welcoming Miller and Agent Upton as well.

Lieutenant Commander Donovan turned back to the Humvee. "Williams, you and Kaili stand guard," he ordered the men. "Keep an eye on the vehicle. I don't want anyone taking off with our ride." Donovan slung his M4 rifle across his back.

"Yes, sir." Seaman Second Class Williams racked the action on the .50-calibre machine gun. He rotated in the turret, his eyes narrowing as he scanned the area.

"*Salam,* Police Chief Hakedam," Agent Upton said, extending his hand warily.

Hakedam shook Upton's hand. Then he gestured at the front door of his small police station. "Please," he said. "You must come inside and have some tea."

Following the Iraqi official, Donovan, Miller, and Upton slowly entered the building one by one.

DEBRIEFING

HUMVEE

HISTORY

The HMMWV, or High-Mobility Multipurpose Wheeled Vehicle is used by the Armed Forces as a troop transporter, command vehicle, ambulance, and for many other functions. The Humvee has armour, making it safer than the jeep it replaced. However, Humvees are vulnerable to automatic weapons fire at close range, as well as IEDs and RPGs.

SPECIFICATIONS

MANUFACTURER: AM General
COST (Unarmoured): $65,000
COST (Armoured): $140,000
PRODUCED: 1984-present
WEIGHT: 5,200-5,900 lbs.
LENGTH: 15 feet
WIDTH: 7.08 feet
HEIGHT: 6 feet
SPEED: 55 mph at max weight, over 65 mph unloaded

FACT

There are at least 17 variants of the HMMWV in service.

1 pound = 0.45 kilograms
1 foot = 0.30 metres
1 mile = 1.6 kilometres

URBAN WEAPONS

IEDs

One of the biggest dangers for US troops in Iraq was improvised explosive devices, or IEDs. Iraqi insurgents placed these homemade bombs along roadways and other high-traffic areas throughout the country. When military transports or innocent civilians made contact with the IEDs, they exploded. The bombs were difficult to detect, so the US military's best solution were "sniffer dogs". These hounds sniffed out IEDs, allowing soldiers to safely dispose of the bombs.

RPGS

RPGs, or Rocket-Propelled Grenades, were a weapon of choice for Iraqi insurgents.

CHAPTER 002

THE PLAN

Police Chief Hakedam and the three US soldiers sat around a small wooden table inside the Iraqi police station. Hakedam poured steaming hot water from a teapot into a fragile cup. He handed it to Lieutenant Commander Lester Donovan and smiled.

"*Shukran*, Chief," said Donovan, taking the cup and blowing on the hot tea.

"I must tell you," Hakedam began. He poured a cup for Agent Upton and Master Chief Miller, and then one for himself. "You are the most respectful Americans we've had here. It is quite refreshing."

"You know why we're here, Chief," Donovan said politely. "What can you tell us about Abdul Kasieem?"

Reaching into his pocket, Hakedam produced a USB memory stick. He handed it to Donovan.

"Ah, yes," said Hakedam, setting his cup on the table. "Kasieem operates in the deep desert on the far side of Quasi, near the Syrian border."

Agent Upton snatched the USB device from Donovan. "Of course," he said. "That's a perfect location for smuggling items over the border."

"Kasieem sells to the highest bidder," said Hakedam. "The potential buyer makes no difference to him. Many have tried to find his weapons, to double-cross him, but none have ever returned. I have heard stories of sliced throats and screams echoing in the deep deserts. Not one man has ever been able to find the main fortress that contains his arsenal of evil. He and his men are ruthless killers who want nothing of Allah's ways. Kasieem is pitiless and cruel."

Hakedam took a cigar from his breast pocket and put it to his lips. Noticing, Donovan reached into his back pocket. He pulled out his small WWI-era trench lighter and flicked it on.

Upton studied Hakedam. He sat back, took a sip of his tea, and then looked at their host intently. After a moment, he said, "Many have said the same of you and your brothers, Hakedam. That you are pitiless and cruel."

Before he could light his cigar, Hakedam threw it to the floor angrily. He slammed his fist on to the table.

WHAM!

"You have insulted my family!" Hakedam shouted.

"No, you have insulted me," said Upton. "We already know everything you're telling us. We know you've had personal dealings with Kasieem in the past."

"The past, yes," proclaimed Hakedam. "I have changed since Americans came and overthrew Saddam Hussein." He slammed his fist on to the table again and again, shaking the cups from their saucers.

WHAM! WHAM!

"Hakedam," began Donovan. The lieutenant commander reached out a hand, trying to calm the police chief. "Don't let the hasty words of this CIA spook get to you. We all know – us soldiers know – what you've built here Hakedam. We know what you've done for the people of Iraq." Donovan glared at Agent Upton.

After a moment, Hakedam smiled. "Yes, yes, you are correct!" he exclaimed, and then he started to laugh. "Please forgive my temper, will you?"

Agent Upton didn't join in the laughter. "What's on this stick?" he asked, holding up the USB device.

Hakedam stopped laughing and looked at Upton, annoyed. "It is the location of his weapons cache and main compound here in Iraq," said the police chief.

Jackpot! Donovan thought. He shot a look over at Master Chief Miller. They both grinned.

"And what do we owe for the honour of this intelligence?" Agent Upton asked suspiciously.

"Nothing," said Hakedam. The police chief picked his cigar off the floor. He dusted it off, placed it in his mouth, and then leant back in his chair with a smile.

Agent Upton glared at Hakedam. "Excuse me?" asked Upton. "You want nothing in return?"

"Consider it ... a good faith gesture," said Hakedam. "You know, for future dealings. If I ever need something, I'll know I can count on Uncle Sal to help me out."

Donovan smiled. He struck his trench lighter again and lit the police chief's cigar. "That's Uncle *Sam*," explained the lieutenant commander.

"Same thing," said Hakedam. He rolled his eyes and jutted out his hand to Agent Upton.

After a short moment, Upton reached out and shook on it. "Done," he said.

*　　*　　*

The US Forward Operating Base was located forty miles east of the Iraqi-Syrian border near the city of Tal Afar. Though Tal Afar had been plagued by terrorist attacks in the past, usually in the form of suicide bombings, the area remained a perfect staging area for the US operation.

The US FOB was close to Kasieem's stronghold. Still, the base was far enough away that military presence wouldn't cause any suspicions to the local people.

"All right, let's go over it again," said Lieutenant Commander Donovan. He stood and pointed at a series of computer screens inside the intelligence tent.

Agent Upton stood, quietly listening, his arms crossed across his chest.

The contents of Hakedam's USB stick were splashed up on the screens. Huddled around the monitors, the three other US Navy SEALs laid out their battle plan. On each of the three screens were satellite photo reconnaissance images of the co-ordinates given to them by Police Chief Hakedam. On the table, each of the men had a hard copy of the map.

"According to the intel provided by Hakedam and our low-orbit spy satellite," Donovan said, "Kasieem's stronghold is camouflaged as a small goat farm five kilometres from the Syrian border. Thermal imaging of the location has confirmed a concrete bunker under the farmhouse itself."

"That's where we assume his weapons cache is stored," said Donovan, pointing to the computer screen. "It's a perfect cover."

The other men shook their heads. The lieutenant knew that, like him, they couldn't believe such a large cache of weapons had been under their noses this whole time.

"We'll HALO in south of the compound and hump it through the dried wadis until we reach the farm," continued Donovan. "Once there, we split into two two-man teams. We enter hot, clearing the main house one room at a time. After we secure the package – code named Viper – we'll exit the way we came in, leaving an IR beacon for the clean-up."

"Are we relying on bunker bombs to take out the cache, sir?" asked Miller.

Donovan nodded. "Yes, Master Chief," he confirmed. "These orders are straight from Admiral Garrow. It's a snatch and grab of the biggest fish, men. We're not there for his toys. That clear?"

"Hoorah!" the men all grunted in unison.

"This'll be Close Quarters Combat, men. Kit out what you'll need for CQB," said Donovan. He looked down at his wrist and checked the time on his grandfather's watch. "We're wheels-up in three hours. Dismissed."

As the others began to file out of the tent, Agent Upton walked over to Donovan. "Not a bad plan, kid," Upton grunted and picked one of the maps off the table. "But a wadi becomes a choke point if things get hot."

Lieutenant Commander Donovan snatched the map away. He didn't have to listen to some CIA agent lecture him on combat. "Don't worry about us," said Donovan. He glared at Upton. "We'll extract through the palm grove if we need to."

The agent shrugged. "Fine," he said. "Sounds like you've got it covered. Just that – well, we've had reports recently of mines hidden in heavy vegetation like this."

"I said, we've got it!" Donovan snapped.

"What's your beef, kid?" asked Upton.

"If I'd followed you back there with Hakedam," said Donovan, "there wouldn't be *any* plan."

"What do you mean?" asked Agent Upton. "Oh, I see. You think my being honest to Hakedam was a mistake? Is that it?"

"That wasn't honesty," said Donovan, raising his voice. "That was plain insulting. You almost cost us the intel. Sir."

"Kid," Upton began. He leant over the desk and started rifling through the stack of paperwork and images. "I've been in this game a long time. The man took a shine to you the second your boots hit the dirt. I saw it as a weakness and exploited it. It was a classic good cop, bad cop scheme."

"You were playing him?" Donovan asked, a bit shocked.

"Donovan, the man is a murderer and a bully," said Agent Upton. "If I don't play his game – you know, stoop to his level of slime – we'd never get anything out of him."

"If you think he's so corrupt, why are we dealing with him?" asked Donovan.

"It's a pendulum here, kid," Upton replied. "Today, Hakedam's in a power position and has what we need. Tomorrow it'll be someone else, and Hakedam will be on the hit list. Either way, we don't get to deal with just nice people in this business."

Upton's schemes didn't sit well with Donovan. He didn't like playing games. He was too aware of all the collateral damage Upton's clever tactics could cause to innocent civilians.

"The Iraqi people are counting on us," said Donovan. "How can we change a world that still relies on bullies and bad guys to make the country run? How is that fair to the people we're trying to protect and liberate?"

"It's not fair," said Agent Upton. "But we're enforcers of policy, not creators. Wanna change the world, kid? Become President. Until then, we all follow orders, so go follow yours."

"You're a jerk," Donovan said angrily as he stormed out of the tent.

Taking a second to breathe, Agent Upton stared at the intel he'd help deliver to the SEALs still projected on the screen. He grinned.

"No arguments there, kid," he said.

DEBRIEFING

US FORCES IN IRAQ

OVERVIEW

US soldiers faced particularly difficult challenges in the Iraq war. Iraqi insurgents used mortars, missiles, snipers, suicide attacks, IEDs (improvised explosive devices), car bombs, gunfire, RPGs (rocket-propelled grenades), and chlorine bombs in war zones and civilian areas alike, creating an unpredictable and deadly environment. Soldiers often found themselves under-protected and without sufficient equipment, leading to high death rates and generally low morale.

FACTS

– A 2010 survey indicated that 4,404 US soldiers died in the Iraq war, with another 31,827 wounded in action.

– On 21st October 2011, President Obama declared that all remaining US soldiers would leave Iraq by 31st December 2011, effectively ending the US's involvement in the Iraq war.

US NAVY SEALS

FACTS

- All SEALs are male members of either the US Navy or Coast Guard.
- SEAL training has a reputation as being the toughest, most rigorous training in the world. The dropout rate for recruits is over 90 per cent.
- Most SEALs spend over a year in training, but it takes nearly thirty months to fully train one Navy SEAL.

HISTORY

The US Navy's Sea, Air, and Land Teams, or Navy SEALs, are the US Navy's primary spec ops force. SEALs are trained to operate on all terrain, making them a very well-rounded force. In the War on Terror, SEAL missions have included counter-terrorism, hostage rescues, and general and special reconnaissance objectives. While the SEALs were originally conceived of as primarily a maritime force, modern-day excursions find them most heavily involved in ground-based missions.

CHAPTER 003

WRECKING CREW

Several hours later, Lieutenant Commander Donovan and his men hit the drop zone near Tal Afar. Like an undiscovered oasis, the palm grove sat in the centre of a valley surrounded by hills of sand. Dried riverbeds, or wadis, led into the oasis like natural roads. All the team needed to do was to follow them.

The edge of the palm grove extended past the mountain range to the south, but was closer to the goat farm. Donovan thought it wise to avoid detection by parachuting in further north and hoofing it.

The moon had set and the desert was pitch black. It was a perfect night to carry out a covert insertion. Noise and light discipline were in effect, so no one spoke. If they needed to speak to one another, they'd use hand signals. Their gear, from straps to ammo pouches, was taped down to prevent any unwanted noises.

Holding up a closed fist, Donovan halted the team. He took a pair of small binoculars from his bag. Night became day as the infrared unit magnified the light and showed him the goat farm in the distance.

The so-called farmhouse was a smaller building than they had planned for. It was nestled right in the far northern end of the grove.

Two Iraqi men patrolled the building, AK-47s in their clutches.

Waving one hand in the air while making fists and walking signals with his fingers, Donovan told the SEALs what to do next.

Quickly and quietly, the squad broke into their two-man fire-teams: Kaili with Williams and Miller with Donovan. They headed towards the farmhouse, their silenced M4 shorties in their hands.

After moving into place, each team crouched in the high cover of the elephant grass on the edge of the palm grove. They waited for their chance to remove the sentries. The grass sighed softly in the night breeze.

One of the guards strode past Master Chief Miller. The sailor was camouflaged in the moonless night. Like a tiger, Miller pounced, wrapping his arms around the man's neck and immediately tackling him to the ground. Miller had expertly incapacitated the guard with a choke hold.

As the other guard passed, Kaili rose from his hidden position. Like Miller had, he blood-choked the Iraqi to the ground, sending him into unconsciousness in seconds. Both men quickly zip-tied the soldiers' wrists and legs.

Gathering back up, Miller with Donovan, Williams with Kaili, they moved towards the house. Team 1 to the back entrance, Team 2 to the side door.

Huddled near the side entrance, Donovan placed a small brick of plastic explosive with a remote trigger on the wooden door's lock. He stepped back. Cradled in his hand was the detonator. He counted down the seconds on his grandfather's watch.

At the rear of the house, Kaili and Williams did the same.

"Three … two … BREACH!" Donovan said.

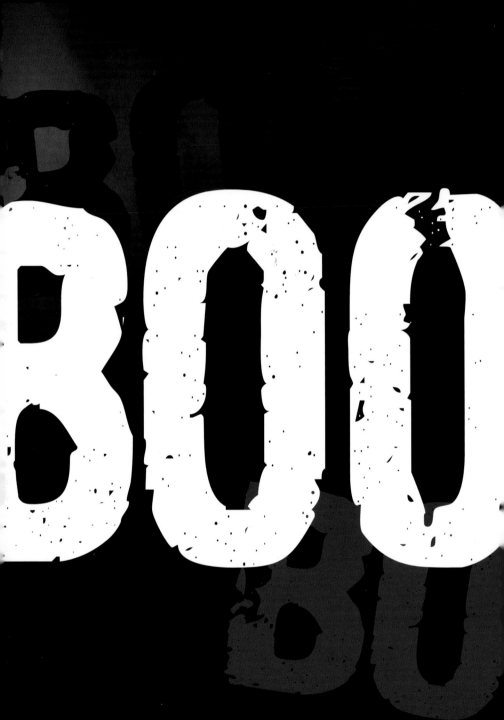

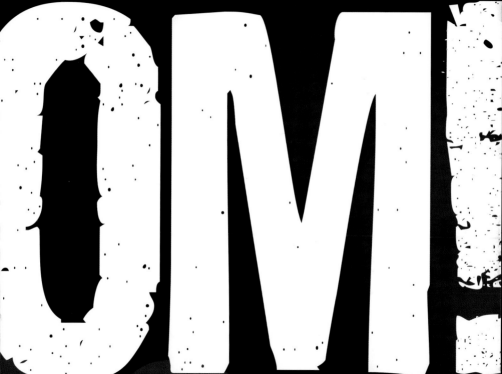

Clicking the detonators almost simultaneously, the SEALs blew open the doors to the small farmhouse. They rushed inside, their M4s up and ready. Donovan entered first and went left. Miller came in behind and broke right.

They were in a living room. The furnishings were minimal and the trappings light. This was purely a flop house, where the men slept after their black-market runs between countries. Small mattresses covered with dirty sheets lay on the floor.

In front of them, two Iraqi men exploded through the doorway, their guns raised and firing.

In a flash, Miller and Donovan opened fire, blasting the men off their feet with short, controlled bursts from their machine guns.

RATATAT! RATATAT!

The SEALs moved deeper into the house.

At the back, Kaili and Williams did the same, their weapons raised. They came through the kitchen, but no one was there.

The men moved cautiously to the next room.

Both teams quickly worked their way to the middle of the house and entered the dining room.

Two waiting gunmen turned and opened fire on Donovan and Miller, causing them to shrink back through the doorway.

OP! POP! POP!

Kaili and Williams came up quickly behind them. Rifles raised, muzzle flash illuminated the Iraqi men's faces as their bodies jerked and fell to the deck. Perfectly placed shots from Fire Team 1 dropped the terrorists in a heartbeat.

"Clear!" Williams yelled as Donovan and Miller entered the room.

At the table, his hands in the air, sat Kasieem.

"I surrender!" Kasieem said.

Kaili threw the man to the floor. He forced Kasieem's hands behind his back and secured them with a zip-tie. Williams scoped the rest of the house.

Master Chief Miller looked over at Donovan and shook his head. "Seem too easy to you?" Miller asked his commanding officer.

Donovan nodded and looked around the room. "Yeah, only six guys and Kasieem?" he said. "Maybe we're missing something."

"Sir!" Williams called.

Donovan turned and ran to his teammate.

*   *   *

Donovan and Williams huddled close to one another, looking at the floor.

In the centre of the room, a trap door was open leading down into the darkness. The two SEALs looked at each other in confusion. "Where's that lead to?" Donovan asked.

"I think it's the access hatch to the weapons cache, sir," Williams said, eyeing the trapdoor nervously.

"Then we'd better ID it," Donovan said. "After you." He gestured at the hole.

"Thanks, sir," Williams said sarcastically. Carefully, he dropped inside the trapdoor.

"Well?" Donovan yelled down to him.

"Can't see a thing, electrics are out," Williams called up from the blackened hole.

"Here," Donovan said, dropping his grandfather's lighter. "What do you see now, Williams?"

A flickering yellow glow shone from the hole in the floor. All Donovan could see were grey concrete steps leading down.

Finally, Williams yelled back. "Nothing, sir! It's just a big, empty bunker."

Confused and angry, Donovan ordered him to come back. They both reunited with the rest of the team.

"What the heck is going on, sir?" Williams asked.

Donovan shook his head. "I dunno, but we did our job and we're outta here," he said. Then the four men, package in tow, moved out of the farmhouse.

AK-47 ASSAULT RIFLE

SPECIFICATIONS

SERVICE: 1949–present
DESIGNER: Mikhail Kalashnikov
WEIGHT: 9.5 pounds
LENGTH: 34.3 inches with fixed wooden stock; 34.4 inches with folding stock extended; 25.4 inches with stock folded
BARREL: 16.3 inches
RATE OF FIRE: 600 rounds/min.
EFFECTIVE RANGE: 330 yd, full-automatic; 440 yd, semi-automatic

1 pound = 0.45 kilograms
1 inch = 2.54 centimetres
1 yard = 0.91 metres

HISTORY

The AK-47 was first developed in the Soviet Union. It was one of the first true assault rifles, and it continues to be widely used today. It remains popular because it has a low production cost, is easy to use, and is very durable. It can be fired as a semi-automatic or full-automatic rifle. In semi-automatic mode, it fires only once when the trigger is pulled. In full-automatic mode, the rifle continues to fire until the rounds are gone or until the trigger is released. A versatile weapon, more AK-47s have been produced than all other assault weapons combined.

NIGHT-VISION DEVICES [NVDs]

HISTORY

As early as World War II, militaries have used night-vision devices (NVDs) in battle. However, first generation NVDs had limited capabilities. They could view objects at no more than a few hundred feet away, and were too heavy to transport. During the Vietnam War, the technology advanced, and some soldiers carried rifles with night vision telescopic sights, called Starlight scopes. Today, US soldiers often wear small, helmet-mounted night vision goggles in darkened combat situations, such as fighting in the urban streets of Iraq.

MODERN WAR

UAVs and NVDs are only a small fraction of the new technologies used during modern wars like the war in Iraq. Lightweight body armour, drone bombers, and specialized tanks allow US troops to be safe and effective soldiers. Even today, however, standard-issue helmets, rifles, and boots, much like those used in WWII, continue to be the most important protection for soldiers on the battlefield.

CHAPTER 004

STEALTH FIGHTER

Outside the farmhouse, Donovan and the men regrouped. Kasieem was still their prisoner.

In his hands, Miller turned on a small infrared LED light and towed it on to the roof of the farmhouse.

"IR's set, sir," he said.

"Good. We're going to extract the way we came in," Donovan said as he pointed at the wadi. "Seahawk's gonna pick us up on the far end where we landed. We'll retrieve our gear and –"

BANG! BANG!

Donovan's shoulder jerked, catching him off balance. He spun 180 degrees and crumpled to the deck.

"Sir!" Miller yelled, kneeling beside Donovan.

Dust clouds puffed up as bullets poured towards them from the wadi.

"Snipers!" Williams exclaimed.

"I'm – I'm okay, Master Chief," Donovan growled as he and the others took cover behind some trees and returned fire.

"Covering fire, Williams!" Miller ordered.

He and Kaili both crouched behind palm trees and fired back at the Iraqis.

POP! POP! POP!

The sound of whizzing bullets filled the air. Firecracker-like pops echoed around them. AK-47 bullets flew through the palm grove. The SEALs were pinned to the ground. They had to formulate a plan.

"Vest took the brunt of it," Donovan said. He coughed.

"Thank God! Last thing I wanna be doin' is carrying you around again." Miller smiled.

"Palm grove!" Donovan ordered. "We'll go north, have the helo pick us up on the other side."

"Right!" Miller said as he stood, weapon in hand.

One by one, the SEALs began peeling off, providing cover for each other as they made their way deeper into the palm grove.

"I count thirty, maybe more, dug in on the south ridge," Kaili said as he loaded his weapon. "We're gonna need some help out here, sir!"

After pulling up a small radio from his daypack, Donovan keyed the handset. "Home Plate, this is Black Mamba," he said. "We have walked into an ambush, I need CAS at 1-8-5 degrees, seven hundred metres up the hillside from my position, over."

Bullets embedded themselves in the tree trunk Donovan was hiding behind.

After a second, Upton's voice came on the line. "Hang tight, Black Mamba. Incoming," crackled the radio.

A small grey shape flew out of the darkness. It swooped past the SEALs and towards the terrorists. In a flash, the UAV Predator drone shot twin Heckfire missiles from under its wings.

KABLAMO!!

Hot red flashes of fire appeared on the mountainside. Suddenly, the shooting stopped.

"Kick butt and take names, Home Plate! And thanks!" Donovan radioed. The SEALs ran deeper into the overgrown cover of thick grass and towering palm trees.

One quick stride at a time, they fled the blazing scene. As they pushed further into the oasis, Lester Donovan suddenly flashed back to his earlier conversation with Agent Upton.

Wait – what was it he said about the foliage? he thought. *Something about –*

Eyes going wide, Donovan turned to his men and shouted, "Freeze!"

It was too late.

In that instant, Kaili's foot came down in just the right spot – a *CLICK* rang out through the night. In a sudden, brilliant flash of yellow and orange, he was propelled five feet into the air.

He'd stepped on a land mine.

The bottom half of his leg was gone, vaporized by the mine's intense heat and fiery explosion. When he landed, he was completely unconscious.

"Kaili!" Williams yelled. He started running.

"No, don't!" Donovan ordered, but Williams ran to Kaili's side anyway. He knelt down by Kaili and began administering first aid.

"No one move! We're in a mine field!" Donovan screamed. He glanced over at Kasieem and could swear the Iraqi was smiling.

Donovan grabbed the radio. "Home Plate, Black Mamba, we are in the middle of a mine field and have casualties. Request immediate extraction, over."

"Negative, Black Mamba," said the voice from the radio.

"What?" shouted Donovan. "We're sitting ducks out here. We need immediate extraction."

"You need to clear the mine field before we can risk a rescue bird," said the radio operator. "Suggest to traverse to the north. MEDIVAC will meet you there, out."

Swearing quietly to himself, Donovan shook his head. "Roger. Out."

"So?" Miller asked.

"They won't risk the helo," said Donovan. "We need to walk out of here on our own."

"Then let the Iraqi take point, sir," Miller suggested as he shoved Kasieem forward.

"No, we can't. If he dies, we have no leads," Donovan said. "Then, even if we were able to get out of this, it would all be for nothing."

"Better than one of us getting blown to heck," Miller shot back.

"No, Master Chief!" shouted the lieutenant commander. "It's not right and I won't do it! I'm not stooping to their level."

A tense moment passed between the SEALs as Donovan racked his brain for a way out of the situation. "How's Kaili?" he asked.

Williams finished applying the tourniquet and looked up at Donovan. "He's bad. We need to get him outta here, sir," Williams said.

"Okay," Donovan said, rising to his feet. "I'll take point."

"No way!" Miller protested, but Donovan waved him off.

"This is the *only* way," Donovan said. "I take point. You all step exactly where I step. We walk out of here and call for extraction on the other side of the grove."

Donovan took a deep breath. He turned north, looking down at the ground, wondering where to start.

The first step, Donovan thought as he lifted his foot off the ground, *is always the hardest.*

His boot was shaking. He could barely hold it up long enough to place it back down.

Finally, he stepped.

Nothing.

Donovan smiled. "Let's move out, Master Chief, and keep him close." He nodded over at Kasieem.

Kasieem was no longer smiling. Now, it seemed he was just as scared to die as the rest of them.

Miller laughed. "Don't worry, sir, I don't think he'll be a problem now."

Miller slowly followed behind Donovan, stepping exactly where the commanding officer's footfalls landed and dragging Kasieem along behind him.

Williams hoisted his Hawaiian teammate over his shoulders in a fireman's carry.

Kaili awoke, groggy and pumped full of morphine, and looked around lazily.

"Williams, be careful, man. . ." he said. "I think there're mines out here." Then he passed out again.

*   *   *

After what felt like a lifetime, the SEALs, moving slowly through the underbrush, came to the edge of the palm grove. A sea of sand spread out before them.

"Home Plate, Black Mamba," Donovan radioed. "We are out of the minefield and en route to the extraction point. Request immediate evac, over."

The radio hissed. "Roger, Black Mamba," Upton's voice said, "you should be able to see them now."

Upton was right. The Seahawk was a small dot on the horizon, but it was on its way. Upton had sent the vehicle out early in anticipation of the SEALs getting to the MEDIVAC point quickly.

All in all, the CIA agent may be a brash, arrogant spook, Donovan thought, *but he's a good man.*

When the helicopter landed, the SEALs rushed forward. A corpsman jumped out, grabbed hold of Kaili, and took charge of him.

One after another, the SEALs boarded, and in an instant the helo powered up and dusted off. The massive rotor blade kicked up storms of sand as it lifted into the air. Its nose dipped, turned west, and disappeared into the sun.

RQ-11A RAVEN UAV

SPECIFICATIONS

TYPE: SUAV (Small Unmanned Aerial Vehicle)
FIRST FLIGHT: October 2001
LENGTH: 36 inches
WEIGHT: 4.2 pounds
WING SPAN: 55 inches
RANGE: 6.2 miles
CEILING: 1,000 feet
CREW: 0

1 inch = 2.54 centimetres
1 pound = 0.45 kilograms
1 mile = 1.6 kilometres
1 foot = 0.30 metres

HISTORY

In modern warfare, unmanned aerial vehicles (UAVs) are essential devices for aerial surveillance and precision bombing. Introduced in 2003, the RQ-11A Raven also had the advantage of its small size. At a little more than four pounds, soldiers can hand-launch the RQ-11 Raven from nearly any location. After the UAV has been deployed, troops can control the vehicle by remote or programme its flight path into a high-tech GPS (Global Positioning System). While in flight, the RQ-11 Raven sends back aerial photographs to troops on the ground.

M4 CARBINE

HISTORY

TYPE: Carbine
SERVICE: 1997–present
WEIGHT: 5.9 pounds
LENGTH: 33 inches
BARREL: 14.5 inches
HISTORY: Since the late 1990s, the M4 carbine has played a major role in US military conflicts, such as the war in Iraq and the war in Afghanistan. This gas-powered, magazine-fed weapon is shorter and lighter than a full-length rifle, making it ideal for urban-combat situations. Able to fire up to 950 rounds per minute, the M4 can provide quick cover-fire and protect troops on the ground.

MK23 PISTOL

For closer range, US special operations forces rely on the MK23 semi-automatic pistol.

CHAPTER 005

WHO'S THE MAN?

The sun was beginning to rise over FOB as Donovan sat alone outside, watching the golden rays of morning break over the horizon.

Though the mission had technically been a success, he felt like a failure. Kaili would live, but he'd lost the lower half of his leg and his career in the Navy SEALs was over.

Immediately after hitting the tarmac, the team had gone through debriefing via satellite link-up with the admirals at SOCOM. Donovan was found non-culpable of any wrongdoing for the incident. But it was his command decision that had got a good man and friend injured and almost killed. He couldn't let go of that.

"Feeling sorry for yourself, kid?" a voice called from behind him.

Donovan turned to see Upton standing there holding, out a bottle of water for him.

"I know, I'm a jerk," said the agent.

"And then some," Donovan snapped. "What do you want?"

"To tell you we debriefed Kasieem. Looks like someone robbed his stash two days before we got there and killed most of his men, which is why no one was really there when you got there." Upton sat next to Donovan and looked out at the rising sun.

"He say who did it?" Donovan asked.

Upton nodded and smiled.

Donovan worked it out immediately and frowned. "Hakedam?"

"Yep, the police chief. We figure he was trying to cut out his competition, which is why he called us in. He gets the guns, we get Kasieem and destroy his operation, and Hakedam becomes the only black marketer in town makin' out like a bandit." Upton laughed.

"Not a bad plan." Donovan chuckled.

"By the way, you did a really good job out there last night," Upton said.

Eyes narrowing, Donovan shot Upton a nasty look. "That is a really crappy thing to joke about," he said.

"No, seriously," Upton said. "Sounds like it got really major out there. Master Chief told me what you did, leading your team out of that mine field."

"We had to get out of there," Donovan replied.

"Took real bravery to not lose it and break down," Upton said. "You showed some great leadership, and whether or not we got played by Hakedam, your guys did the job perfectly."

"It shouldn't have gone that way," Donovan said, glancing over at Upton. "I missed something you were trying to tell me because I let my anger and ego get in the way. And because of that, a good man was almost killed."

"You're right," Upton said.

"Don't sugarcoat things much, do you?" Donovan said sarcastically.

"Nope," Upton said. "Things can go wrong even if you do everything right. We got the bad guy, and we didn't lose anyone. Sometimes that's all you can ask for."

"It's still not right," Donovan said. "If I had only listened, that kid would still be walking."

Upton stood and nudged Donovan with the water bottle. Donovan took it. "At least he's still breathing," Upton said. "And next time, you'll know better."

Upton walked off then, leaving Donovan alone with his thoughts.

Donovan stood and stared at the water bottle in his hand. Water. It was a precious thing out here, in a country in the middle of the sand. Precious, like a pair of legs to stand on. Like being able to hold up your head for a mission well done. Like leading your men to safety even though your heart is pounding in your chest, and you're as frightened as a little kid.

He took a drink. As the first light of a new day crossed his face, Lieutenant Commander Donovan sat, pondering his future.

DEBRIEFING

SH-60 SEAHAWK

SPECIFICATIONS

FIRST FLIGHT: 12th Dec 1979
ROTOR: 53 feet, 8 inches
LENGTH: 64 feet, 8 inches
HEIGHT: 17 feet, 2 inches
WEIGHT: 15,200 pounds
MAX SPEED: 207 mph
CRUISE SPEED: 168 mph
CEILING: 12,000 feet
CREW: Two (pilot and electronic warfare officer)

1 foot = 0.30 metres
1 inch = 2.54 centimetres
1 pound = 0.45 kilograms
1 mile = 1.6 kilometres

HISTORY

The US Navy replaced older, often heavier, helicopters with SH-60 Seahawks during the 1970s. Twin turboshaft engines and deployment possibilities make Seahawks popular aircraft for surface warfare, anti-submarine warfare, and search and rescue missions. The typical SH-60 Seahawk carries a crew of three to four people and can deploy from and land on nearly any surface, including destroyers, cruisers, or assault ships. Each Seahawk helicopter also carries several torpedoes, missiles, and a machine gun.

THE END

WITHDRAWAL

In late February 2009, newly elected US President Barack Obama announced an 18-month transitional period of withdrawal for combat forces. Around 50,000 troops were left behind in order to train the new, democratic Iraqi government's security forces. On 31st August 2010, President Obama declared that the war in Iraq was officially over, and that "the Iraqi people now have responsibility for the security of their country". However, even though the combat missions had been declared over, fighting still occurred across much of Iraq.

SADDAM HUSSEIN

The invasion eventually led to the capture of Saddam Hussein, who was later tried in an Iraqi court. On 30th December 2006, he was executed by the new Iraqi government for crimes against humanity.

FACT

On 21st October 2011, President Barack Obama announced that all US soldiers would leave Iraq by the new year, which would end the US mission in Iraq. To date, no WMDs were located in Iraq during the invasion.

EXTRAS

ABOUT THE AUTHOR

M. ZACHARY SHERMAN is a veteran of the United States Marine Corps. He has written comics for Marvel, Radical, Image, and Dark Horse. His recent work includes *America's Army: The Graphic Novel, Earp: Saint for Sinners,* and the second book in the SOCOM: SEAL Team Seven trilogy.

AUTHOR Q&A

Q: Any relation to the Civil War Union General William Tecumseh Sherman?

A: Yes, indeed! I was one of the only members of my family lineage to not have some kind of active duty military participation - until I joined the US Marines at age 28.

Q: Why did you decide to join the US Marine Corps? How did the experience change you?

A: I had been working at the same job for a while when I thought I needed to start giving back. The biggest change for me was the ability to see something greater than myself; I got a real sense of the world going on outside of just my immediate, selfish surroundings. The Marines helped me to grow up a lot. They taught me the focus and discipline that helped get me where I am today.

Q: When did you decide to become a writer?

A: I've been writing all my life, but the first professional gig I ever had was a screenplay for Illya Salkind (*Superman* 1-3) back in 1995. But it was a secondary profession, with small assignments here and there, and it wasn't until around 2005 that I began to get serious.

Q: Has your military experience affected your writing?

A: Absolutely, especially the discipline I have obtained. Time management is key when working on projects, so you must be able to govern yourself. In regards to story, I've met and been with many different people, which enabled me to become a better storyteller through character.

Q: Describe your approach to the *Bloodlines* series. Did personal experiences in the military influence the stories?

A: Yes and no. I didn't have these types of experiences in the military, but the characters are based on real people I've encountered. And those scenarios are all real, just the characters we follow have been inserted into the timelines. I wanted the stories to fit into real history, real battles, but have characters we may not have heard of be the focus of those stories. I've tried to retell the truth of the battle with a small change in the players.

Q: Any future plans for the *Bloodlines* series?

A: There are so many battles through history that people don't know about. If they hadn't happened, the world would be a much different place! It's important to hear about these events. If we can learn from history, we can side-step the mistakes we've made as we move forward.

Q: What's your favourite book? Favourite movie? Favourite video game?

A: My favourite book is *The Maltese Falcon* by Dashiell Hammett; I love a good mystery with hard-boiled detectives! As for movie, hands-down it's *Raiders of the Lost Ark*. It is a fantastic story of humanity winning out over evil and the characters are real people thrown into impossible odds. Lots of fun! As for games, there are waaaay to many to mention, but I love sci-fi shooters and first person games.

ABOUT THE ILLUSTRATORS

Josef Cage is a Filipino artist based in Manila, Philippines. He currently works in advertising, creating storyboards for television commercials. He dreams of doing comics full-time someday. His most recent work is a comic book called *TRESE*.

Marlon Jay G. Iligan is an artist, son, and brother. His fascination with the written word and storytelling led him into a career as a comic book colourist. He believes stories are conversations between the creator and their audience, and he feels blessed to be a part of this discussion.

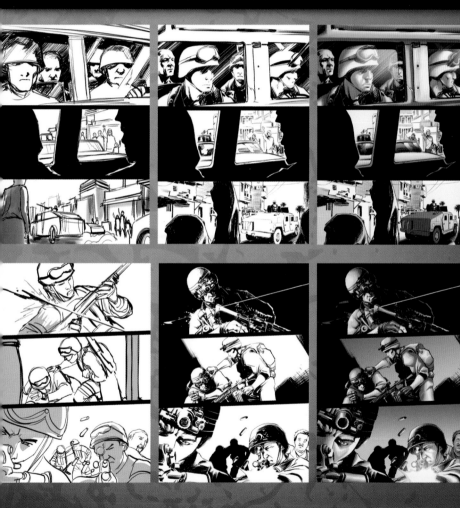

A CALL TO ACTION

WORLD WAR II

BLOODLINES
DEPTH CHARGE

WORLD
★ WAR II ★

M. ZACHARY SHERMAN

KOREAN WAR

BLOODLINES
DAMAGE CONTROL

KOREAN
★ WAR ★

M. ZACHARY SHERMAN

During World War II, British Intelligence discovers a German U-505 submarine anchored off the coast of Denmark. Stashed on-board are invaluable codebooks, keys to deciphering the enemy's communications. To secure the documents, a British commando and US Army First Lieutenant Aaron Donovan must team up, sneak aboard the enemy submarine, and get off alive!

During the Korean War, a US Army cargo plane crashes behind enemy lines, and soldiers of the 249th Engineer Battalion are stranded. Facing a brutal environment and attacks by enemy forces, Private First Class Tony Donovan takes action. With spare parts and ingenuity, he plans to repair a vehicle from the wreckage and transport his comrades to safety.

VIETNAM WAR

BLOODLINES
EMERGENCY OPS

VIETNAM
★ WAR ★

M. ZACHARY SHERMAN

During the Vietnam War, Captain
Anne Donovan of the US Army
Nurse Corps heads to the front
lines. Along with a small medical
unit, she'll provide aid to the soldiers
at Hamburger Hill. When the battle
intensifies and the deaths multiply,
this talented rookie nurse must try
to reconcile her role as a healer
with the never-ending blood bath
that is war.

IRAQ WAR

BLOODLINES
HEART OF THE ENEMY

IRAQ
WAR

M. ZACHARY SHERMAN

During the war in Iraq, Lieutenant
Commander Lester Donovan of
the US Navy SEALs must capture
a known terrorist near the border
of Syria. It's a dangerous mission.
Land mines and hostile combatants
blanket the area, yet Donovan is
undeterred. But when the mission
goes awry, this gung-ho commander
must learn to keep his cool if he's
going to keep his men alive.

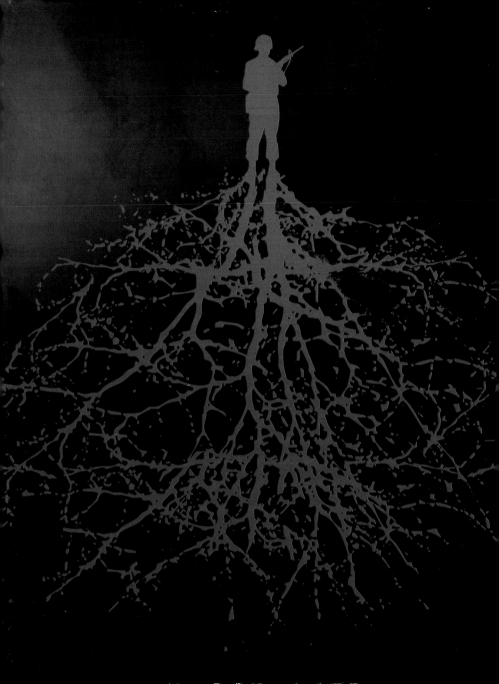

BLOODLINES